Me and My Mummy

LETTERS TO DAN GREENBURG
ABOUT THE ZACK FILES:

From a mother in New York, NY: "Just wanted to let you know that it was THE ZACK FILES that made my son discover the joy of reading...I tried everything to get him interested...THE ZACK FILES turned my son into a reader overnight. Now he complains when he's out of books!"

From a boy named Toby in New York, NY: "The reason why I like your books is because you explain things that no other writer would even dream of explaining to kids."

From Tara in Floral Park, NY: "When I read your books I felt like I was in the book with you. We love your books!"

From a teacher in West Chester, PA: "I cannot thank you enough for writing such a fantastic series."

From Max in Old Bridge, NJ: "I wasn't such a great reader until I discovered your books."

From Monica in Burbank, IL: "I read almost all of your books and I loved the ones I read. I'm a big fan! *I'm Out of My Body, Please Leave a Message*. That's a funny title. It makes me think of it being the best book in the world."

From three mothers in Toronto: "You have managed to take three boys and unlock the world of reading. In January they could best be characterized as boys who 'read only under duress.' Now these same guys are similar in that they are motivated to READ."

From Stephanie in Hastings, NY: "If someone didn't like your books that would be crazy."

From Dana in Floral Park, NY: "I really LOVE I mean LOVE your books. I read them a million times. I wish I could buy more. They are so good and so funny."

From a teacher in Pelham, NH: "My students are thoroughly enjoying [THE ZACK FILES]. Some are reading a book a night."

From Madeleine in Hastings, NY: "I love your books...I hope you keep making many more Zack Files."

THE ZACK FILES™

Me and My Mummy

By Dan Greenburg

Illustrated by Jack E. Davis

GROSSET & DUNLAP • NEW YORK

For Judith, and for the real Zack,
with love—D.G.

I'd like to thank my editor
Jane O'Connor, who makes the process
of writing and revising so much fun,
and without whom
these books would not exist.

I also want to thank
Emily Sollinger and Tui Sutherland
for their terrific ideas.

Text copyright © 2002 by Dan Greenburg. Illustrations copyright © 2002 by Jack E. Davis.
All rights reserved. Published by Grosset & Dunlap, a division of Penguin Putnam Books
for Young Readers, New York. GROSSET & DUNLAP and THE ZACK FILES are trade-
marks of Penguin Putnam Inc. Published simultaneously in Canada. Printed in the U.S.A.

Library of Congress Cataloging-in-Publication Data is available.

ISBN 0-448-42633-1   A B C D E F G H I J

Chapter 1

I've never gotten along with older kids. Then I met a kid who was three thousand years old, and he was one of the nicest kids I ever met.

OK, maybe I'm getting ahead of my story.

My name is Zack, and I'm in the fifth grade at the Horace Hyde-White School for Boys in New York City. My mom and dad are divorced, and I spend half my time with each of them. The half that I spend with my dad is always when weird stuff happens to me, like the time I'm going to tell you about.

Dad had just bought me a new bike for my birthday. A twenty-four speed mountain bike. It was the coolest thing you've ever seen. Well, actually, you haven't seen it. But if you had, you'd think it was cool. Anyway, I took it on a pretty long ride in Central Park. When I came home, Dad said to take my bike down to the basement and put it in our storage space.

I have to tell you that the basement in our apartment building is one of the three creepiest places in the world. Everybody in the building stores junk down there. There are spiderwebs all over the place. The lights usually aren't working. In winter the furnace makes creepy noises. And a kid named Cyril in the building told me an old janitor died down there—either died or was killed, I forget which. Cyril says at night you can sometimes hear his ghost moaning.

So anyway, there I was in the basement. I didn't hear the dead janitor moan. But no sooner did I get my bike into our locker, then I saw something interesting in the storage bin next to ours. It belongs to our neighbor, Mrs. Taradash—the one who has all these weird stuffed squirrels and rabbits in her apartment. What I saw in her space was a battered-up old wooden box with a funny shape. I thought it was a case for a bass violin. I've always wanted to learn how to play a musical instrument. If Mrs. Taradash had an old bass violin that she wasn't using, maybe she'd let me learn to play it.

Mrs. Taradash's bin wasn't even locked.

I went inside it. Don't ask me why because it was plenty creepy down in the basement. And once I got inside, I saw that the case was definitely not for a bass violin. Now that I was up close, I could see that the box was in the shape of a body. Don't ask me why. But I decided to open it. It was tough to get the cover off the body-shaped box. Once I did, I wished I hadn't. It was too dark in the basement to see much, but it was light enough to see what was inside the case. It wasn't a bass violin. It looked like a human body! A not-very-big human body, about my size—and completely wrapped in cruddy old bandages from head to toe.

Suddenly I knew what I was looking at. I had just opened a mummy case! And underneath all those cruddy old bandages was a real live mummy—actually, a real *dead* mummy. The thought made my skin crawl. But as creeped-out as I was, I was also pretty interested. It didn't smell as bad as I thought it would. It smelled a little like dried hay. I leaned closer to get a good look at the mummy. That was when it moved its arms.

I completely freaked out. I screamed and slammed the cover of the mummy case. Then I got the heck out of there. I didn't even wait for the elevator. I ran up the stairs, screaming the whole way.

Chapter 2

"Calm down, Zack," said Dad. "What are you so excited about?"

"A mummy!" I shouted. "A mummy is in the basement!"

"What? Somebody's mom is in the basement?"

"No, no, a mummy! A dead person wrapped in bandages! And it's *alive*!"

"You're not making sense, Zack. How could there be a mummy in the basement? And how could a dead person be alive?"

I grabbed Dad's wrist.

"I'll show you. C'mon! Hurry!"

"What's the rush?" Dad asked. "If it's a dead person, it's not going anywhere." Dad was *not* taking me seriously. So down in the basement, I dragged Dad over to Mrs. Taradash's bin. I pointed at the mummy case. I pointed at the open mummy case.

"There."

"Wow," said Dad. "It *is* a mummy case. Mrs. Taradash told me she went to Egypt a couple months ago. This must be something she brought back as a souvenir."

"When can we ask her about it?"

"Not for a few months," said Dad. "A few days after she got back from Egypt, she left for a trip to India."

I should tell you that I don't get along too well with things from Egypt. Once on a class trip to the Temple of Dendur I got scratched by an Egyptian cat goddess and started turning into a cat. But that's another story.

"Let's take a look inside that mummy case," said Dad. "I'm sure Mrs. Taradash won't mind." He walked up to the mummy case. I couldn't look. "Zack?" said Dad. "There's nothing here. The mummy case is empty."

"What?" I said. I walked over to the mummy case and looked inside. He was right. The mummy was gone!

"Dad, you've got to believe me," I said. "The thing was here three minutes ago. I swear!"

Then I noticed something. A little sign on the front of the mummy case.

"What's that?" I said. I pointed to the sign. "Can you read what it says?"

Dad leaned close to the mummy case and squinted at the sign.

"Oh, it's, uh, nothing," he said. He seemed a little nervous.

"Nothing? How could it be nothing?"

"Oh, it's just some kind of a warning or something," he said. "I wouldn't take it seriously."

"Let me see it," I said.

I leaned close to the mummy case and squinted at the sign. Here is what it said:

WHOSOEVER DISTURBS

THE SLEEP OF THE MUMMY

WILL BE CURSED.

THIS NOT A JOKE.

Chapter 3

That night, I just couldn't get to sleep. At midnight, I went into the kitchen.

"What's wrong? Why can't you get to sleep?" Dad asked.

"Are you kidding me?" I said. "Didn't you see what that sign said? 'Whosoever disturbs the sleep of the mummy will be cursed.' Who do you think disturbed the sleep of the mummy? Me."

"I wouldn't take it seriously," said Dad. "There's no such thing as a curse."

"Oh no?" I said. "What about the time

we were in Hawaii and I was cursed by that volcano goddess?"

"OK," said Dad. "That was a curse. But it was different."

"How was it different?" I asked.

"Well, for one thing, it was in Hawaii. For another thing, it was a volcano goddess, not a mummy. And for another thing, uh..." Dad's voice trailed off.

We looked at each other. Dad shrugged.

"I really don't think this curse was like that curse," he said.

When I finally got to bed, I insisted that Dad put a night-light in my room. I haven't needed a night-light in my room since I was a little boy. I kept thinking about the mummy I saw. I wondered where it was now. It had to still be in the building somewhere. Walking around. Trying to find the person who opened the mummy case. Trying to find *me*.

Just as I was about to fall asleep, I heard something at the front door, scratching to get in.

"Dad!" I screamed.

Dad rushed into my room right away.

"Zack, what it is?"

"The front door!" I shouted. "Something's trying to get in!"

Dad started to open the door.

"Wait!" I said. "We need protection!"

Dad grabbed a broom. All I could find was a frying pan. With broom and frying pan in front of us, we carefully opened the front door.

There was nothing there. But on the door were scratches. Deep scratches.

Chapter 4

"We've got a mummy loose in our building," I announced at school the next morning.

"Oh yeah?" said Andrew Clancy. "Well, we had a zombie loose in our building last week. The week before that we had a werewolf."

Andrew Clancy always tries to top anything anybody says. Nobody takes him very seriously.

"How do you know you have a mummy

loose in your building?" asked Spencer Sharp. He's my best friend and the smartest kid in the school.

"Because I saw it," I said. "I opened this mummy case, and there it was, all wrapped in these yucky bandages. It looked like a kid or something. And then it started to move."

"What did you do?" asked Spencer.

"You kidding me?" I said. "I ran. Why? What would *you* do?"

"I would have stayed to observe its behavior."

"Yeah, right," I said.

"My parents wanted to buy me a mummy for my birthday," said Vernon Manteuffel. "It was either that or a tree house. I chose the tree house. It has cable TV, two bathrooms, and a sauna."

Vernon is this really rich kid in our class who sweats a lot. He's always trying to impress us with how rich he is. Nobody takes him very seriously, either.

Mrs. Coleman-Levin walked into the class and sat down at her desk. She is our homeroom teacher and my science teacher as well.

"Good morning, boys," she said. "Please pass your homework up the aisle to my desk."

"Mrs. Coleman-Levin," said a kid named Ben Lerner, "There is a mummy loose in Zack's apartment building."

"Is this true, Zack?" asked Mrs. Coleman-Levin.

"Yes, ma'am," I said. "I saw it moving. Then I ran away. And when I came back it was gone. Have you ever heard of a mummy doing something like that?"

"Rarely," said Mrs. Coleman-Levin. "If you have any further contact with this mummy, Zack, do let us know."

That night as I was getting ready for bed, I felt a little less nervous. It had been more than twenty-four hours. Nobody had seen or heard anything about the mummy. Nothing bad had happened to me. Maybe there wasn't a curse after all. Maybe the mummy had gone to another building in another neighborhood in another country. I turned off the light and went to sleep.

That night I had weird dreams. I was in Vernon's tree house, in the sauna. Suddenly, a zombie walked in. He wanted to use the sauna and he kicked me out. Then the tree house turned into the Temple of Dendur. I was looking at a painting of a mummy. The mummy in the painting started unwrapping itself. Underneath, it was a werewolf. The werewolf smelled like dried hay. Then, gradually, I woke up.

You know how sometimes when you

wake up you think you're still in a dream? That's how I felt. In fact, I could still smell the dried hay. As my eyes grew accustomed to the dark, I saw something so creepy I stopped breathing. There was somebody standing at the foot of my bed!

Oh, please, I thought, *let it be my dad!* But if it was my dad, why did he smell like dried hay? And why was he so short?

"Dad," I whispered, "is that you?"

There was no answer. With my heart beating in my throat, I slowly reached for the switch on my bedside lamp. I turned it on.

Yikes! Standing at the foot of my bed was the mummy!

I screamed.

"Oh, please, kind sir, do not be afraid," said the mummy. Its voice was the voice of a kid. A kid with a very hoarse voice. A voice that hadn't been used in thousands of years.

"W-who are you?" I said when I could speak. "W-what are you doing in my room?"

"My name," said the mummy, "is Ikhnaton. Ikhnaton the Second, to be exact. But you can call me Icky."

"Icky?" I repeated.

"Yes," said the mummy. "Kind sir, can you tell me where I am?"

"You're in Manhattan."

"I have not heard of such a place, kind sir," said the mummy. "In what part of Egypt is this Manhattan?"

"Manhattan isn't in Egypt," I said. "It's in the state of New York. In the United States of America. In North America. You've been...asleep for quite a while."

"Asleep?" said the mummy. "For how long a time?"

"Pretty long."

"But this is terrible!" said the mummy.

"My homework is overdue! My instructor will *kill* me!"

I gulped. This conversation was beyond weird. But somehow I wasn't so scared anymore. How could I be scared around someone who was so polite and kept calling me "kind sir"?

"I don't think you need to worry about your instructor anymore," I said.

"Indeed?" said the mummy. "How can you be sure?"

"Trust me," I said. "By the way, my name is Zack."

"It is pleasant to meet you, Zack," said the mummy. "But I am frightened and hope you can help me."

"*You're* frightened?" I said. "Of what?"

"Someone is following me. I don't know who it is or what they want. They hide in the shadows. It makes me very uneasy."

"Well," I said, "I can't imagine who'd be following a mummy."

"Nor can I. Also, I have not eaten for quite a few years, kind sir. May I kindly ask you for some food?"

"Sure," I said. "Come on in to the kitchen."

I took the mummy into the kitchen.

"By the way," I said. "there was a sign on your mummy case that said whoever disturbed the sleep of the mummy would be cursed. What, exactly, is the curse?"

"Oh, you know," said the mummy. "The usual. Things begin falling off the body of the person who was cursed. Fingers, toes, noses, that sort of thing."

Yikes! I felt dizzy. I grabbed the kitchen counter and held on tight.

"Y-you're saying my fingers and toes are going to start falling off now?" I asked.

"Oh, my. No," said the mummy. "*You* didn't disturb my sleep. I was awake already when you opened my mummy case."

Whew! What a relief *that* was.

I wasn't sure what mummies ate, so I fixed him a peanut butter and jelly sandwich. The clock on the wall said 2:10 A.M. Boy, what an hour to be making a peanut butter and jelly sandwich for a mummy in my kitchen! I handed him the sandwich.

"I thank you from the bottom of my heart, Zack," said the mummy. "What is this?"

"A peanut butter and jelly sandwich," I said.

"Ah," said the mummy. "Even before tasting it, I know I shall love it."

He took a bite, chewed it, and swallowed it. Then he threw up. That was the point at which Dad walked into the kitchen, rubbing his eyes.

Then he stopped, stared, and rubbed his eyes some more.

"Can somebody please tell me what a mummy is doing throwing up in my kitchen at 2:10 A.M.?" Dad asked.

"Dad, this is the mummy I was telling you about," I said. "His name is Ikhnaton. Icky, this is my dad."

"Delighted to make your acquaintance," said Icky. He threw up the rest of the peanut butter and jelly sandwich.

"Icky said he was hungry, Dad. So I made him a peanut butter and jelly sandwich. I guess he's not used to American food. Don't worry, I'll clean it up."

"Good," said Dad. He turned to go. "One less thing for me to do. He can sleep in your room tonight, Zack."

I guess by now Dad doesn't get so fazed by the sudden appearance of a mummy. He wasn't nearly this calm when Zeke, the kid from the alternate universe on the other side of our medicine cabinet, showed up.

"I don't think Icky sleeps," I said. But Dad was already on his way back to bed.

Chapter 5

I was right. Icky wasn't at all interested in sleeping. All he wanted to do was talk. He kept me up all night, talking. He said he was scared. He kept going on about how someone was following him. He didn't know what they wanted.

He said he was lonely. He missed his mom and dad. He wanted to get back to Egypt and look for them. He had a headache. He had a stomachache. I told him that if he didn't feel better in the morning, we'd take him to the doctor.

The next day was Saturday. Icky was still feeling icky, so Dad made an appointment with the doctor. (Not that Dr. Kropotkin was much help the time I became invisible.)

It was a bright, sunshiny day. The second we got out of the apartment building, Icky took one look at the sun and fell to his knees.

"Icky, what are you doing?" I asked.

"Praying to Aton, the sun god," he said. He pointed to the sun.

"You're praying to a ball of hot gases ninety-three million miles away?" I asked.

"What?"

"Never mind," I said.

Dad flagged down a cab.

"A chariot!" said Icky, looking at the cab. "A chariot without horses! How is that possible?"

"I'll explain it on the way to the doctor's office," I said. "Just get inside."

Just before we all squeezed into the backseat of the cab, I saw something out of the corner of my eye. Somebody in dark clothes, ducking around the corner of our building—maybe the person Icky thought was following him.

"Icky, I just saw somebody duck around the corner."

"Where?"

"Right over there." I pointed. He looked. But whoever it was had disappeared.

"Zack, I am frightened," said the mummy. "Why are they following me?"

"Hey," said the cab driver. "Are you guys getting in or what?"

"Better get in the cab," I said.

We climbed inside. The cab driver looked at Icky in his rearview mirror. If he seemed surprised to see a mummy in the back seat of his cab, he didn't show it.

It's pretty hard to surprise a New York cab driver.

Dad gave him the doctor's address and the cab took off.

When we got to Dr. Kropotkin's office, people in the waiting room took one look at Icky and moved to the other side of the room.

"My friend was in an accident," I explained. "That's why he's all bandaged up."

People gave us these very forced smiles and moved even farther away.

Finally, it was our turn. We took Icky into Dr. Kropotkin's office.

"Well, well, well," said Dr. Kropotkin. "Good morning. And whom do we have here?"

"This is my friend Icky," I said. "He's got a headache and a stomachache."

"And a bad pain in my chest," said Icky.

"A pain in your chest?" said Dr.

Kropotkin. "Well then, Icky, let's listen to your heart a moment."

Dr. Kropotkin put the earpieces of his stethoscope into his ears. He pressed the end of the stethoscope to Icky's chest. He frowned.

"Hmmm," said Dr. Kropotkin. "That's strange. I'm not getting any heartbeat at all here. Come over to the X-ray machine, Icky."

Icky walked over to the X-ray machine. Dr. Kropotkin stepped behind a screen that protects you from radiation and turned on the X-ray machine.

"Hmmm," said Dr. Kropotkin. "This is even stranger. Icky, did you know you have almost no internal organs?"

"Oh, that is quite right, kind sir," said Icky. "I nearly forgot. In Egypt when they turn you into a mummy, they remove nearly all of your internal organs."

"A-ha," said Dr. Kropotkin. "Well, that explains it."

He turned off the X-ray machine.

"So what can we do about the pains in Icky's head, his stomach, and his chest?" I asked.

"For pains," said Dr. Kropotkin, "I usually prescribe aspirin. But taking aspirin isn't safe unless the patient is over sixteen. Tell me, Icky, how old are you?"

"Three thousand three hundred and twenty-one," said Icky.

Dr. Kropotkin nodded seriously.

"In that case, Icky," he said, "take two aspirin, drink plenty of liquids, rest in bed, and call me in the morning. Oh, and you might want to change those bandages." Dr. Kropotkin reached for some bandages on his shelf and gave us about a dozen rolls.

When the three of us got out on the

street, people took one look at Icky and started freaking out.

"Zack," said Icky, "why do they behave so strangely when they see me?"

"I guess they just aren't used to seeing mummies on the street," I said. "As soon as we get home, I'll lend you some of my clothes."

We took a cab back home. When we entered the lobby, I thought I saw somebody in the shadows. Maybe I was just getting spooked.

"Did you see that?" said Icky. "It's the person who has been following me."

"I didn't see anything," said Dad. "Did you, Zack?"

"Maybe," I said.

Now *I* was getting scared. Who could be following Icky? And what could they want? Whoever it was, they sure weren't up to anything good.

When we got back into our apartment, Dad gave Icky two aspirin. I gave him a pair of my jeans, a sweatshirt, and sneakers. To cover up his bandaged face, I gave him a Yankees baseball cap and a pair of sunglasses.

"How do I look, Zack?" Icky asked.

"Cool," I said. "Very cool."

"I feel warm, however."

"I meant you look really good," I said.

"Then why am I so unhappy?" he asked.

"Is it because you miss your mom and dad?"

Icky nodded.

"OK," I said. "I know just the person who might be able to help you. I'll call her right now and see if we can visit her."

Chapter 6

When Mrs. Coleman-Levin opened the door to her apartment, there was strange music playing inside. I thought I could hear flutes and harps and stuff. It sounded kind of sad. Mrs. Coleman-Levin was wearing a long purple-and-gold robe.

Mrs. Coleman-Levin is not only our science teacher, but she works weekends at the morgue. I figured she'd know a lot about dead bodies and mummies.

"Hi, Mrs. Coleman-Levin," I said. We walked inside.

"Good afternoon, Zack," said Mrs. Coleman-Levin. "And this must be Icky."

Something was burning. It didn't smell bad, though.

"Yes," I said. "Mrs. Coleman, this is Ikhnaton the Second."

"Ikhnaton the Second?" said Mrs. Coleman-Levin. "Why, I believe I know your parents."

"You do?" said Icky. He sounded really excited.

"Well, not personally, of course," she said, "but I've certainly read about them in history books."

Icky looked sad again.

"Icky's father was Ikhnaton the First, a great king of Egypt," said Mrs. Coleman-Levin. "And his mother was Queen Nefertiti, which makes Icky a prince. They lived in Egypt in the Eighteenth Dynasty. That's about 1300 B.C., or 3,300 years ago."

"That is all correct," said Icky. But he seemed even sadder than before.

"Icky's father told his people that Aton, the sun god, was the only god," said Mrs. Coleman-Levin. "Not everybody liked that."

"But Aton *is* the only god," said Icky.

"Well, Icky," said Mrs. Coleman-Levin, "in this country we allow people to worship any god they choose."

"Is there something burning in here?" I asked.

"That's incense," said Mrs. Coleman-Levin. "I thought it might make Icky feel more at home. So tell me, boys, how can I help you?"

"Well," I said, "Icky really misses his parents. I thought you might be able to help him find them."

Mrs. Coleman-Levin raised her eyebrows.

"Zack, may I see you a moment in my study?" she asked.

"Sure," I said.

"Excuse us for a moment, Icky," she said.

Mrs. Coleman-Levin took me into her study. On the walls were all kinds of stuff from her travels. Masks from Africa, voodoo stuff from Haiti, the jaws of a Great White shark, shrunken human heads—stuff like that.

"Zack," she said, "it doesn't seem as though Icky knows his parents are dead."

"I don't think Icky even knows *he's* dead," I said, "although he did tell Dr. Kropotkin that when they turn you into a mummy they take out all your internal organs."

"That's partly true," said Mrs. Coleman-Levin. "Actually, the Egyptians left in the heart, because they believed it was the source of thinking and wisdom. But they removed the brain because they thought it was completely useless." She smiled a wicked smile. "I'll bet you'd like to know how they removed the brain," she said.

"Not really," I said.

"They stuck a sharp tool up the dead person's nostril to scrape it out," she said. "I call it the ultimate nose-picker."

"Thank you for sharing that," I said.

Suddenly, I had the spooky feeling that we were being watched. I looked at the window. Was that a face, peering in at us?

"What are you looking at?" asked Mrs. Coleman-Levin.

"I thought I saw a face at your window," I said.

"Zack, we're on the tenth floor here," said Mrs. Coleman-Levin. "You must have imagined it."

"You're probably right," I said. "I'm

probably a little jumpy because Icky thinks he's being followed. Anyway, where was I? Oh, yeah. Icky says he wants to go back to Egypt. But we don't have enough money to pay for his plane fare."

"And it would be so different from the Egypt he knew 3,300 years ago," said Mrs. Coleman-Levin. "He probably wouldn't be any happier there than he is here."

"Which is not much," I said. "Do you have any ideas at all of what we can do with him?"

"It's always awkward when the dead become undead," said Mrs. Coleman-Levin. She thought a moment. "Tell me," she said, "don't you have a great-grand-father who died and came back as a cat?"

"You mean Maurice," I said. "Yeah, he's living down in Florida now with a lady named Bernice."

"Well, the cat was a sacred animal to the Egyptians. Why don't you give Maurice a call and see if he has any ideas?"

I phoned Great-Grandpa Maurice as soon as we got back to Dad's.

"Zack!" shouted Maurice. He always talks into the phone way too loudly. "How great to hear your voice!"

"It's great to hear yours, too," I said. "How's Bernice?"

"Terrific," he said. "Why are you calling me, bubbeleh? Are you turning into a cat again?"

"No, no, nothing like that," I said. "I'm calling to help a new friend of mine. His name is Ikhnaton the Second. He's a mummy. We found him in our basement."

"So what's the problem?"

"He's lonely," I said. "He misses his

parents, Ikhnaton the First and Queen Nefertiti. I thought you might know them, being a dead person yourself."

"When did they die?"

"About 1300 B.C."

"Hey, kid, give me a break," said Maurice. "I don't know *everybody* who's dead. Besides, they kicked the bucket almost 3,200 years before me."

"OK," I said. "Well, it was just a long shot."

"Come to think of it, I do know a guy who knows a guy who said he met Nefertiti at a party once. I'll give him a call."

"You think he might know where she is?" I asked.

"Who knows?" he said. "Hey, I'll give it a shot."

"Thanks, Great-Grandpa Maurice," I said.

When I hung up I told Icky about my

conversation. He seemed sadder than ever. To cheer him up, I turned on the TV. He seemed really amazed that so many little people could fit into the TV cabinet. I raced through about a dozen channels, and stopped when I saw a mummy.

Icky took one look at the mummy and almost jumped out of his bandages.

"Father!" he screamed.

My dad came running into the living room.

"You calling me, Icky?" Dad asked.

"No!" he said. "Not you, kind Dad, sir. *My* father!" He pointed to the TV screen. "My father is inside of that box! But why is he so small?"

Icky ran around to the back of the TV and tried to pry it open.

"Icky, stop," I said. "That box is a television. There's nobody inside of it. It's just pictures of people. Pictures that move."

"Icky," said Dad. "What makes you think that mummy is your father?"

"It is! It is!" he screamed. "Do you not think I can recognize my own father?"

We watched the program awhile. It was a documentary about Egyptian mummies on the Discovery Channel. And Icky was right. The mummies they were talking about were Ikhnaton the First and Queen Nefertiti. They said both mummies were now part of an Egyptian exhibit at the Los Angeles County Museum.

"Dad," I said, "Icky's parents are in Los Angeles! Is there any way you could possibly take us there?"

"Yes, kind Zack's kind father," said Icky, "could you kindly take us to Los Angeles, whatever that is?"

"Whoa!" said Dad. "It costs money to go to Los Angeles. And money is something I don't have a lot of right now."

Just then I heard something right outside our front door. It sounded like a fart. I threw open the front door in time to see somebody race down the hall.

"Dad! Icky!" I shouted. "Whoever's been following Icky just farted and ran down the hallway!"

Dad, Icky, and I ran after whoever it was. When we turned the corner at the end of the hallway, we saw him. You're not going to believe who it was. The butler of Vernon Manteuffel, the rich kid in school who sweats a lot!

"What the heck are *you* doing here?" I demanded.

Vernon's butler turned around to face us. He looked pretty embarrassed.

"Sorry about the, um, gas," he said. "Master Vernon sent me. He's grown bored with his tree house. He's decided he wants a mummy after all."

"Is that so?" I said. "Well, Vernon can't have *this* mummy."

"Actually," said the butler, "I don't even think it's the mummy itself that Master Vernon wishes. I believe he wants the little gold amulets and scarabs he's heard are usually wrapped in mummy's bandages."

"Yeah?" I said. "Well, maybe Master Vernon hasn't heard about the mummy's curse."

"The m-mummy's curse?" said Vernon's butler. "What is that, pray tell?"

"Things start dropping off whoever messes with the mummy's treasures," I said. "Fingers, toes, noses—other little things like that."

"Oh, dear me, just look at the time," said Vernon's butler, without even looking at his watch. "Well, it's been lovely chatting with you, but I must return home and draw Master Vernon's bath."

Vernon's butler raced down the hallway to the stairs. We went back inside.

"Dad," I said. "What if you could get an assignment from some magazine to write about Icky searching for his mom and dad? Do you think we could afford to go to Hollywood then?"

"Hmmm," said Dad, stroking his chin. "You know something? That isn't such a bad idea at all, Zack. I'll bet I could even get my editor to pay for the trip."

Icky started jumping up and down with joy. I don't know if you've ever seen a mummy jumping for joy, but it's pretty interesting.

Chapter

7

The flight to California was cool. Well, it was once we convinced Icky to get onto the plane. He was sure it was the belly of a huge silver falcon. But when he finally got on board, he thought it was awesome to fly so high above the clouds. He spent most of the flight listening to music on his earphones and looking out the window because Dad wouldn't let him try any of the airplane food, and when we flew over Las Vegas, he went nuts.

"A pyramid!" he screamed, pointing at the ground. "Is this not Egypt?"

Dad looked where Icky was pointing.

"That's not a real pyramid, Icky," said Dad. "It's made of glass, not stone. It's a Las Vegas hotel called the Luxor."

Icky didn't say anything. I could tell he wasn't buying it.

When we landed in Los Angeles, Icky begged us to go straight to the museum. Dad said sure. We took a cab from the airport. But when we got inside the museum, we couldn't find Icky's parents' mummy cases anywhere.

A guard in a dark blue uniform and a little cap was snoozing behind a velvet rope.

"Excuse me," I said. "Where is the mummy exhibit with Ikhnaton the First and Queen Nefertiti?"

The guard jolted awake, then pretended he hadn't been sleeping at all.

"That exhibit isn't available to the public at the present time," he said. "It's in the basement for repairs."

"But, kind sir, it is really quite important that we be able to see it," said Icky. "We have come all the way from Manhattan in North America to do so."

The guard looked at Icky. If he was surprised to see a mummy talking to him, he didn't show it.

"That exhibit isn't available to the public at the present time," he said.

"Look," said Dad, showing the guard his press card. "I'm writing a story about mummies for *Universal Geographic Magazine.* It's really important that we get to see the mummies."

"That exhibit," said the guard slowly, looking angrily at Dad, "isn't available at the present time."

We couldn't leave here without seeing

Icky's mom and dad—we just couldn't. I was getting desperate. If only I could think of some way to impress this guy. Then I remembered nasty old Professor Fufu, who was Head of Exhibits at the Rosencrantz Museum of Natural History in New York. Fufu hated me for refusing to sell him a baby dinosaur and for feeding junk food to his Neanderthals. But that's another story.

"We've brought a message for your museum director from our very close friend, Professor Fufu of the Rosencrantz Museum in New York," I said.

"Professor who?" said the guard.

"Fufu," I said. "Please tell your director. We'll wait right here."

The guard sighed and went to talk to the museum director.

"Who is Professor Fufu?" asked Icky.

"A guy who hates my guts," I said, "but this just might work."

Icky wandered off to look at an exhibit of Egyptian scarabs. A couple of minutes later, the guard returned with the museum director. The director was a guy in a white lab coat. He had a shaggy gray beard and messy white hair.

"This here is the director of the museum, Dr. Hans Horstplop," said the guard.

"Glad to meet you, Dr. Horseplop," I said.

"Good to meet you, Dr. Horseplop," said my dad.

"That's *Horst*plop," said the director. "The guard said you had a message from Professor Fufu?" Then Icky wandered back. The director took one look at him and almost fainted. "Mother of pearl!" said the director. "What is *this*?"

"Oh, let me introduce you," I said. "This is his royal highness, Prince Ikhnaton the Second. Icky, say hello to Dr. Horseyplop."

"I am pleased to meet you, Dr. Horsey-plop," said Icky.

"That's *Horst*plop," said the director. He took a magnifying glass out of his pocket, dropped to his knees, and began examining Icky all over. "Mother of pearl!" he kept repeating, "I cannot believe what I'm seeing here!"

"Well, you might as well believe it," I said, "because it's true."

"This is a genuine Eighteenth Dynasty mummy," he said. "Where did this come from?"

"Mrs. Taradash's basement bin," I said.

"What?" said Dr. Horstplop.

"Never mind," I said. "Icky has come all the way from New York to see his parents. Can we go down to the basement now and have a look at them?"

"Yes," said Icky. "I would be most appreciative."

"Mother of pearl!" said Dr. Horstplop. "Of course, of course. Come right this way."

So Dr. Horstplop led us down to the basement of the museum. It was packed with junk, just like the basement in Dad's building, except that the junk in Dad's basement was pretty much rusty bicycles and broken lawn furniture, and the junk here was mostly dinosaur bones and woolly mammoth skeletons.

Way off in the corner I could see two huge mummy cases, covered in gold paint and precious stones. Icky saw them, too. He raced over to them and started babbling.

"Mother! Father!" said Icky. "It is I, Ikhnaton the Second, your son! Can you hear me? Can you give me some sign that you can hear the sound of my voice?"

"Is there any way that you would

consider letting this mummy stay here at the museum?" whispered Dr. Horstplop.

"That would be something you'd have to work out with Icky himself," I said.

"And with Mrs. Taradash," said Dad.

"Who?" asked Dr. Horstplop.

Just then we heard an amazing creepy sound. The covers of both the large mummy cases began to slowly creak open.

"Mother of pearl!" said Dr. Horstplop.

So Icky got reunited with his parents. And Dr. Horstplop fainted and had to be revived by paramedics. And Dad did his magazine assignment about Icky's reunion with his mom and dad, which paid for our trip.

It was kind of tough saying good-bye to Icky. Even though he was an older kid, I really got to like him. Just before we left,

Icky gave me a golden scarab. It was wrapped up in his bandages, just like Vernon's butler said.

Icky and I still keep in touch. He says he's pretty happy in Los Angeles. His parents moved to a nice place out on the beach in Malibu. And he's trying to audition for a part in the latest *Mummy* movie. At least I *think* that's what he wrote me. His letters are a little hard to understand. They're on papyrus and they're written in hieroglyphics, so I can't be sure.

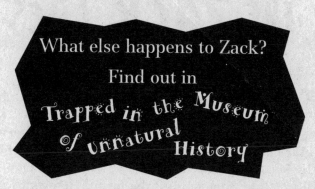

What else happens to Zack?
Find out in
Trapped in the Museum
of Unnatural History

I turned my head in all directions. I heard strange grunting noises. And then something grabbed me from behind!

Whatever grabbed me was pretty strong. No matter how hard I struggled, I couldn't get away from it. I heard a whoosh, like a fire starting up, and then I saw a torch. Somebody had lit a torch and was bringing it over to look at me.

The somebody came closer. Its face was wide and hairy and apelike. It had deep-set eyes. It was a Neanderthal! I had stumbled into the Neanderthal exhibit! Holy guacamole – the Neanderthals were alive and they'd taken me prisoner!

THE ZACK FILES™

Out-Of-This-World Fan Club!

Looking for even more info on all the strange, otherworldly happenings going on in *The Zack Files*? Get the inside scoop by becoming a member of *The Zack Files* Out-Of-This-World Fan Club! Just send in the form below and we'll send you your *Zack Files* Out-Of-This-World Fan Club kit including an official fan club membership card, a really cool *Zack Files* magnet, and a newsletter featuring excerpts from Zack's upcoming paranormal adventures, supernatural news from around the world, puzzles, and more! And as a member you'll continue to receive the newsletter six times a year! The best part is—it's all free!

✄ ---

☐ Yes! I want to check out *The Zack Files*
   Out-Of-This-World Fan Club!

name: _____ age: _____

address: _____

city/town: _____ state: ___ zip: _____

Send this form to: Penguin Putnam Books for
Young Readers
Mass Merchandise Marketing
Dept. ZACK
345 Hudson Street
New York, NY 10014